THIS BOOK BELONGS TO

_____

WITH LOVE FROM

_____

I dedicate this book to all our fur babies that have given us years of joy, snuggles, slobber kisses, side-eye, roll-on-the-floor laughter, exercise, muddy paw prints, protection, companionship, and everlasting love. This is for you Betsy, Sydney, Emma, Gianna, Lola, Samson, Boris, and of course, Comet and Cosmo.

—Candace

À ma petite maman Lu.
Ta fille qui t'aime tant.

—CB

ZONDERKIDZ

Candace's Playful Puppy

Copyright © 2020 by Candache, Inc.
Illustrations © 2020 by Christine Battuz

This book is also available as a Zondervan ebook.

Requests for information should be addressed to:
Zonderkidz, 3900 Sparks Dr. SE, Grand Rapids, Michigan 49546

ISBN 978-0-310-76902-6

Art direction and design: Cindy Davis

printed in Italy

20 21 22 23 /IMG/ 23 22 21 20 19 18 17 16 15 14 13 12 11 10 9 8 7 6 5 4 3 2

Candace's Playful Puppy

WRITTEN BY **Candace Cameron Bure**

ILLUSTRATED BY **Christine Battuz**

Candace woke up and peeked out her window. The sun was shining. The sky was blue. And a gentle breeze blew through the leaves on the trees.

Finally! The day Candace had been waiting for had arrived.

Candace's mother was taking her to adopt a dog!

Candace's pet hamster, Harry, wasn't too happy about it. But Candace promised Harry that having a dog would be fun.

The first stop was the pet store. Candace pulled out her shopping list. Then she chose a special bed, bowls for food and water, a leash, and LOTS OF TOYS!

"Just a few!" said her mother.

Harry didn't have anything to say.

At the animal shelter, Candace couldn't believe what she saw.

There were big dogs and little dogs. Short-haired dogs and furry-all-over dogs. White dogs. Black dogs. Yellow dogs. And one little brown-and-white puppy with more spots than the polka-dotted pillow on Candace's bed.

All of the dogs needed a nice home and someone to take care of them. But when Candace picked up the spotty little puppy, his floppy ears perked up and his long tail thumped so fast that Candace knew he was the dog for her.

"I'll name you Freckles," she said. And just like that, Candace and Freckles were friends.

Candace waited patiently while Mom filled out the paperwork.

She cleaned up when Freckles made a mess and didn't say, *"Ewww!"*

And when the nice lady at the shelter gave her a book on how to train a puppy, Candace tucked it under her arm and made a promise to be the best dog mommy ever.

In the car, Candace tried to hold Freckles on her lap. But Freckles was more interested in sticking his head out the window to enjoy the breezy day.

At home, Candace showed Freckles his new toys. The only thing Freckles wanted to play with was Harry.

"Candace, it's your job to train Freckles," said Candace's mother. She reminded Candace that teaching a new puppy how to behave was going to be hard work.

But Candace wasn't worried. Everything she needed to know was right there in the book.

The next day, Candace invited her best friend Sophie Rose to help with puppy training. They took Freckles into the backyard.

"Sit!" Candace commanded Freckles.

Sophie Rose pointed to the ground.

But Freckles didn't want to sit.
He jumped on Sophie Rose . . .

chased a squirrel . . .

and rolled around in the soft green grass.

"He just wants to play," laughed Sophie Rose. Candace didn't think it was so funny.

She tried again. This time Candace held out a treat and told Freckles to sit.

"Good puppy!" she said when Freckles sat.

Candace smiled happily while Freckles gobbled up the treat.

Then he dashed off, running loop after loop around the backyard while Candace and Sophie Rose chased after him.

When Candace finally caught Freckles, she plopped down on the ground. "Puppy training is a lot harder than I thought it would be."

"Don't worry," said Sophie Rose. "I'm sure it will get easier every day."

But days, weeks, even months passed, and puppy training wasn't always easy.

Sometimes, when Candace told Freckles to sit … or stay … or roll over, Freckles would sit … or stay … or roll over. But most times, Freckles wanted to chase squirrels … dig in the backyard … or roll around in the leaves.

Candace was frustrated. And so was Harry.

"Candace, you must stay faithful and dedicated even when it's hard," said her mother.

And it was hard.

At night, Freckles didn't like to sleep in his special crate.

Every time Candace
gave Freckles a bath, he
made a big, soapy mess.

He even chewed up Candace's
training book.

Candace had to remind
herself that she couldn't give up

One morning at breakfast, Candace's mother gave Candace a leash and said, "Candace, please take Freckles for his morning walk before it starts to rain."

Candace put on her boots and her coat. She put Harry in her pocket.

But as soon as they walked outside, Freckles dashed off, his leash trailing behind him.

Candace and Harry searched everywhere for Freckles. They asked everyone if they'd seen a little brown-and-white spotted puppy. But Freckles was nowhere to be found.

"All I wanted was to be a great dog mommy!" sobbed Candace. "And now Freckles is lost."

Even Harry was sad.

Candace and Harry said a prayer that they would find poo Freckles. They just had to stay faithful and keep looking.

The sun was starting to set, but Candace wouldn't give up. She and Harry continued to look for Freckles.

Candace and Harry turned a corner. They heard a bark, then saw Freckles running toward them!

"Freckles!" cried Candace. He was wet and muddy when he jumped on Candace and Harry, but they'd never been happier to see him. And Freckles looked happy too.

At home, Candace gave Harry and Freckles a long, bubbly bath, and she didn't even mind when Freckles shook suds and bubbles all over the bathroom.

Then the three of them curled up in Candace's bed. She hugged her pets and gently patted their soft, furry heads.

"Candace, I know it isn't always easy, but you're a great dog mommy because of your faithfulness to always love and care for Freckles," said her mother. Then she gave Candace a hug and said she was proud of her for not giving up.

Candace smiled. Being a great dog mommy wasn't always easy, but she was never, EVER going to give up.

The next day, Candace got a new book on how to train dogs. She kept working to teach Freckles to sit and stay and roll over.

Most days Freckles did what Candace taught him to do.

But some days Freckles just wanted to play and have fun.

And some days … so did Candace.